LAUNDROMAT GIRL

Story & Illustration
by **Patsy Stanley**

Laundromat Girls

Here's to the Laundromat Girls—
Laundromat Oracles,
Zen Spinners of the Cycles of Wash,
keepers of soap, steam, and second chances.
Spin, spin, spin...
Careful now—don't let the socks fall in.
Slosh, slosh, scrub, scrub, scrub.
Rain outside. Snow outside.
Lightning strikes—
Yikes!
A true Laundromat Girl just nods.
She's seen worse.
Laundromat Girls have washed christening gowns
and funeral dresses, school uniforms,
waitress aprons, factory jeans,
and one good suit that only came out
for weddings and burials.
They've scrubbed away baby spit,
garden dirt, engine grease,
coffee stains, blood, tears,
and lipstick on a collar
that was better left unexplained.
Every stain tells a story.
True Laundromat Girls never ask.
They just know.
The washing machines gossip enough.
Leota's Hopeful Laundry Soap.
Soap, soap, soap. Rinse, rinse, rinse.
Pretty soon, everything smells like lavender,
or mint, or another chance.

LAUNDROMAT

Laundromat Girls are
Rinse Mystics,
Fabric Whisperers,
Tumble Psychics.
They know that white never stays white,
that socks always lose their partners,
that every family owns towels
older than their grandchildren,
and that life keeps piling up on your washables
whether you're ready or not.
They know most washables come clean eventually.
Not all things. Some grief has to be worn thin.
Some heartaches only soften after nine hundred
washes.
Still...
Every Tuesday, every Thursday, someone comes in
carrying a week's worth of troubles
in a blue plastic basket to be washed away
An hour later, she walks out lighter.
Maybe it wasn't the washing. Maybe it was being
among women who know. So here's to the
Laundromat Girls—washing a little worry out of the
whole damn world, one load at a time.
Now let's get down to business!
  There are seven hundred and sixty-seven ways to
learn Laundromat Zen. Every one of them works.
Some people learn it beside a creek, scrubbing over
smooth rocks. Others learn it in downtown
laundromats while waiting for the dryer to stop
thumping. Some learn it hanging sheets between
apartment windows, where the wind decides whether
they'll smell of sunshine, garlic bread, fish, or all
three.

The great Zen Masters of Laundry—Sudsy Pope, Detergent Grant, and Soapy Dillon, known simply as *The Big Three*—insist that baptismal wisdom is found somewhere between the wash cycle and the rinse. They even wrote a dictionary explaining such lofty matters as droopy knits, permanent press, top-loading enlightenment, and what to do when your deodorant gives up before you do.

Not everyone is called to Laundromat Zen.

Some folks wear wrinkled shirts without a care. Others sleep on scratchy sheets.

But if you've ever believed that clean clothes could somehow make the whole world feel a little more hopeful...well...you may already be on the path. Which brings us to a Laundromat Girl named Leota...

Leota wasn't just a girl who worked in a laundromat—she became a Laundromat legend! Leota has cats. Leota needs a laundromat to find her Zen. Her cats, being cats, are already Zen Masters.

This is her story...

Leota didn't begin life as the famous Laundromat Girl everyone came to know. She began life as a frightened little girl on the run with her family, carrying more worry than belongings and learning early that clean clothes, a warm blanket, and a kind smile could sometimes save a person's spirit.

Years passed.

Little by little, basket by basket, wash after wash, Leota became a living legend. Folks came from all over just to use her laundromat, buy a box of **Leota's Hopeful Laundry Soap**, and leave feeling somehow lighter than when they arrived.

Some folks claimed it was the soap.
Others said it was the way Leota greeted everyone
like an old friend. The truth was probably a little of
both.

Her faithful cats stayed beside her through it all.
They were older, wiser, and far more accomplished at
Laundromat Zen than Leota ever hoped to be. They
didn't need washing machines, dryers, soap, or rinse
cycles.

A true Zen Cat can find perfect contentment on a
warm windowsill, an empty cardboard box, the top of
a humming dryer, or a sunny patch of sidewalk.
Leota often said her cats taught people how to wash
clothes.

Her cats quietly taught her how to live.
And that is how a little girl who once had nowhere to
belong grew into the most famous Laundromat Girl
in the whole world.

Laundromat customers loved **Leota's Hopeful
Laundry Soap**:

- "Guaranteed to remove grass stains, gravy,
  and ordinary despair."
- "Now with extra Hope."
- "Not responsible for missing socks."
- "Works best when accompanied by kindness."

Now, on to Leota's story...one that begins without
hope. But ends with success!

LAUNDROMAT

Leota grew up on the outskirts of cities where mushrooming hovels and houses full of unwashed, traveling miscreants lived. Of course, Leota and her family didn't always live in places as nice as hovels and houses while she was growing up. They lived in shacks, at off-limits campsites, and sometimes in old cars from the 30's up on blocks where water was scarce.

Leota's few clothes came from the thrift stores or from giveaways. When she grew old enough to choose her own clothes, Leota chose black. Plain and simple.

No silly pinks or froo froo purple throwaways. No frilly topped faded socks. No tossed out sneakers. No shocking lime green tights or shy blue, shrunken sweaters, washed in water too hot, then thrown away.

Her mother finally gave up and gave in. Leota could wear anything she wanted to; her mother had too many other things to worry about, like why her brother Larry-Lace-His-Shoes couldn't tie a bow.

Leota turned six and was fast becoming too wise too early from constantly wearing black. Her process of worrying about sinking into either a Goth life or into dire depression was interrupted one day when she watched a woman use a tin scrub board to scrub clothes clean in a tin washtub full of soapy, sudsy, pine smelling water.

She watched the clothes go in dirty and come out clean. She was amazed, astounded, and at last, hopeful about something.

She stole the scrub board that smelled like pine and hid it behind a tree near their campfire.

She tried the scrub board out. It cleaned and rippled and made sounds that she forever remembered. It was very satisfactory...

It was with her and the miscreants when they moved on again. And again.

The years passed. Leota wore more tattered black and searched out laundry lessons and found at least one in most of the places they lived.

She learned the diameters and shades of clothes lines and their stretch-ability. She learned how to tie the proper clothes line knots.

She learned to be creative and innovative when it came to where to string up a clothesline. *"Better than stringing myself up or another person."* she thought grimly as she learned to tie bow line, clove hitch, and figure eight knots. None of the rest of her family gave a damn about clean clothes or the wonders of pine scented belongings. Just Leota.

When Leota was eight, she found an empty laundry box discarded by the road. She picked it up, examined it, and took it home to her mother to smell.

"What is that smell?" she asked.

"Lavender." her mother said briefly.

Leota hid the box under the scrubbing board.

"Pine, mint, and lavender."she whispered to herself, smiling. After awhile, Leota was first to find the clean water supply in each place they lived.

undroMat

One day she noticed a wringer washer sitting on a porch near the latest shack they were living in, and though she was usually shy and quiet, she was bold.

They discussed laundry methods and products. Leota learned from the lady of the house.

"Use the kind that always gives you a gift, like a towel or a dish, they are the best!" the lady stated firmly, handing Leota an unopened box of washing powder with a small, brand new towel tucked inside it as a parting gift when Leota came to tell her they were moving on.

Leota learned about fabric softeners, bluing, laundry cycles, which clothes to wash in hot, warm or cold, the uses of borax, baking soda, and bleaches. She learned how long to soak different kinds of stains, how to use dyes in the washing machine, and vinegar.

She wrote down the recipes for cleaning the different kinds of smut out of clothes that women told her about in a small journal she kept hidden from her large, noisy family.

She became adept at recognizing the different textures and fragrances of commercial laundry powders. Some smelt of lemon, others of bleach or flowers. By the time she was eighteen, she had become an old maid and an old soul who knew one thing for sure: She knew how to do laundry. She had become a Laundry Expert.

She knew all about textiles and how to cleanse them; the rest followed. She began organizing her secret journal into categories.

The more she washed, the more her family
became cleaner miscreants who still snubbed
her. At last she became an outcast whose
ministrations they endured.

For a while, washing her family's clothes was
enough. Then the loneliness settled in. Leota began
dreaming of a better life. She began making secret
plans. She wandered through thrift stores,
searching the crowded racks for black dresses. Black
was practical. It hid stains, matched everything, and
looked respectable even when it had belonged to
someone else first.

She pinned back her dark hair, bought one tube of
bright red lipstick, and tucked it carefully into her
handbag.

Then she began working on something no one else
knew about. She filled scraps of paper with notes,
crossed out ingredients, and started over again. Little
by little, she created the formula for a special
laundry soap.

It wasn't meant to make people rich.

It was meant to make hard lives feel a little fresher, a
little softer, and a little more hopeful.

Leota guarded the recipe carefully.

One day, she believed, it would carry her out into the
world.

Leota left her family and moved to a nearby Big
City.

No one said goodbye.

But Leota had a plan.

She wandered the streets of the Big City until
she found an alley behind a Laund-O-Rama.

Do you Mind?
cat seen?
YES?
yes?
WHAT!
Privacy here?
contemplating is serious business!

She settled into a hidden corner of the alley and set up housekeeping. Leota had learned some things from her miscreant relatives, such as how to pick the kind of back door locks that were on the Laundromat. She also knew how to make laundry soap boxes. The next morning, when the Laund-O-Rama opened and the customers poured in, Leota was standing inside, wearing a black dress, holding small boxes of Hopeful Laundry Soap in her hands.

Hopeful Laundry Soap was a product Leota had created from the advice of all of the industrious users of scrub boards and wringer washing machines that had passed through her life, especially that first one. Leota still had that tin scrub board and treasured it.

The customers thought she was an attendant; so did the boy who opened the doors every morning for the absentee owner. They bought the Hopeful Laundry Soap from her as she moved smoothly among them, giving advice about settings and applications of fabric softeners.

The Laund-O-Rama customers found themselves telling Leota about their lives. They spoke of things she'd never heard of, and she traveled with them through their stories. She listened and learned, and they felt heard in their hasty, busy, Big City lives.

Besides, Leota's Hopeful Laundry Soap smelled heavenly, and their clothes were cleaner, brighter and folded more quickly with her help than ever before! They loved that she wore formal wear.

Her black dress put them on their best behavior and gave them respect for themselves. Some of them began to entertain the idea that doing laundry might not be just a mundane task. They requested her name and discreetly handed her a tip before they left. At the end of her first day at the Laund-O- Rama, Leota bought herself dinner with their generous tips before she returned to her temporary lodging in the alley behind the Laund-O-Rama.

Days went by, and Leota sold more and more Hopeful Laundry Soap to people and listened to their stories.

After awhile, the Laund-O-Rama became so crowded that the boy who locked and unlocked the doors morning and night, told the absentee owner about it.

The owner came to see what was going on. Incognito, but with an eye always towards profit, he watched Leota as she graced his Laund-O-Rama. Instead of kicking her out, he decided to sell her laundry soap on a bigger scale and split the profits with her. He wasn't all that shrewd, but he knew clean clothes when he saw them. He counted a bunch of new customers who came in with dirty clothes and left with them clean. Business was booming.

The owner installed a vending machine in the Laund- O-Rama and went away. Leota filled the vending machine with Hopeful Laundry Soap boxes every morning and sometimes several times a day. Soon there were long lines of people trying to buy more and more of it. Who could resist a laundry soap that smelled that good and cleaned 234% better than any other laundry soap?

ndroMAt

That's what the package said, so it had to be true.

The owner of the Laund-O-Rama came back again and tried to get Leota to tell him the ingredients of her laundry soap.

But she'd learned more from her miscreant relatives than he bargained for. For he was a miscreant, too, and she recognized it. He could not persuade her to tell him the secret ingredients for the wonderful laundry soap that had almost everyone in the Big City standing on their ears.

Finally they struck a deal and he went away. And so, Leota became the proud Leader of the Laund-O-Rama and her Hopeful Laundry Soap went into production and became available on grocery store shelves throughout the Big City!

She was a laundry success at last! Her dream had come true! It was time to design a heroine pin that proudly proclaimed "Leota is a True Laundromat Girl!" a pin that would perfectly complement her sleek black dresses.

Leota left the alley behind and moved into a second floor walkup above the Samplesing Deli across the street where she could keep an eye on the Laund-O-Rama and eat pastrami, too. No more detergent hands. No dyed in the wool lone nomadic socks calling out to her to find them as she passed the Laund-O-Rama door.

To fill her evenings, Leota adopted six alley cats and took cello lessons from the colossally talented Mr. Dubo, who lived just around the corner from the Laund-O-Rama.

The six alley cats had all arrived in the Big City from somewhere else. They were drifters, strays, wanderers, and survivors. One had ridden into

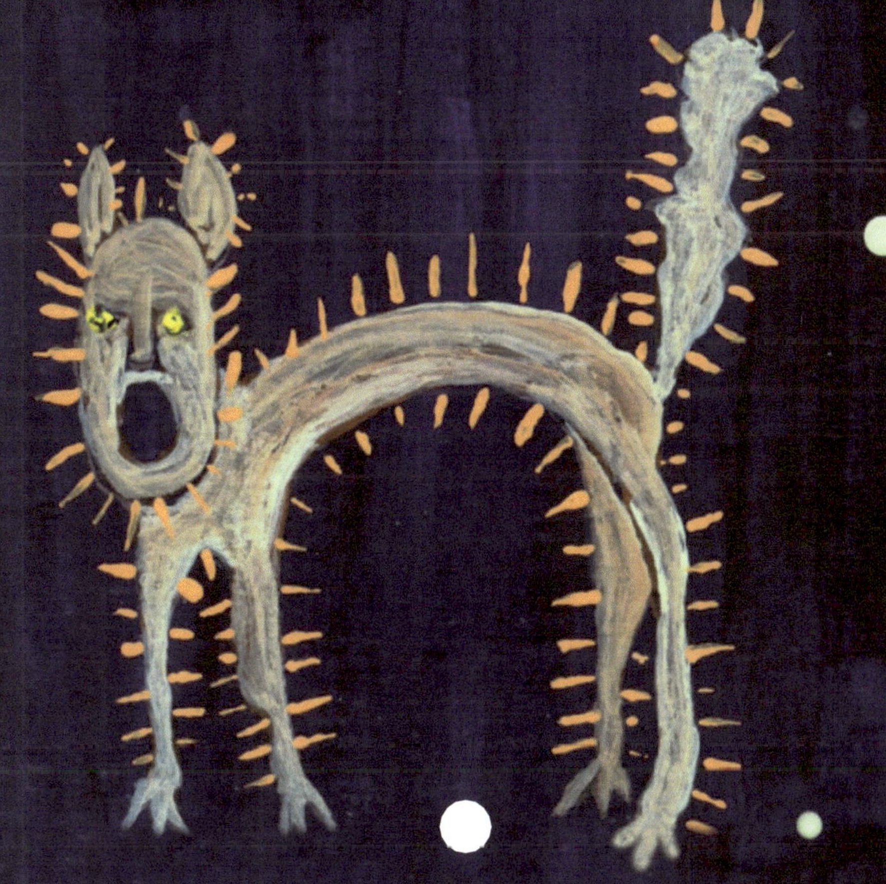
Cactus
Cat
cat
Zen

town in the back of a produce truck. Another had followed the railroad tracks. One simply appeared one rainy Tuesday and never left. Leota gave them names, warm places to sleep, and supper every evening. In return, the cats gave her company. Mr. Dubo gave her music. Between the cello, the cats, and the steady hum of the washing machines, Leota found that loneliness had a way of shrinking, little by little.

For a long while, Leota kept herself busy with the cats. They needed names. They needed flea baths. They needed reminding that the kitchen table was not a mountain and the curtains were not something to climb. One by one, they settled into her little apartment and quietly made themselves at home. Leota loved them for asking so little.

In the evenings, after the dishes were done and the laundromat had grown quiet, she would sit by the window with a cup of tea and think about her family. She tried to remember all the reasons she'd left. There had been plenty. Enough to fill a lifetime.

But something peculiar kept happening. Just when she'd gathered up the hardest memories, one of the good ones would come wandering in, uninvited. The good memories kept interrupting the bad ones. They sprang up like dandelions pushing through cracks in the sidewalks of the Big City. No matter how much concrete life poured over them...
There they were.
Bright.
Stubborn.
Growing anyway.

Her father's high, mild laugh when one of her
brothers told a joke so funny he couldn't catch his
breath.
Her mother humming while stirring the never-ending
pot of pinto beans on yet another homemade stove.
A brother chasing a chicken he was trying to steal,
while the chicken somehow stayed one step ahead of
him.
White snowball bushes blooming beside the rickety
back steps.
A sister handing her a wild pink rose.
The smell of clean sheets drying on the clothesline.
The sound of rain drumming on an old tin roof.
A warm biscuit passed to her by her mother before
anyone else noticed.
The good memories kept interrupting the bad ones.
Leota finally decided memories were like laundry.
No life ever came out all white or all black.
Most lives were washed together...
  The six cats constantly encouraged Leota to keep
up her courage.
"The past is over," they told her. "Ours is, too."
But Leota worried about the future instead.
  Every night, the six cats wandered the alleys,
rooftops, fences, and back stairways of the Big City.
By morning, they returned with full bellies, dusty
paws, and fresh bits of wisdom gathered beneath
moonlight.
They shared everything they had learned.
That tomorrow always comes.
That a warm windowsill is a blessing.
That a cardboard box can be a palace.

Laundromat

That a little kindness is never wasted.
That there is no sense mourning yesterday when the morning sun is already warming your whiskers.
The cats believed these things completely.
Leota wanted to.
But she wasn't ready to listen. Not yet. Yes. Leota was trapped by memories!

Well, cats don't *learn* Laundromat Zen—they already know it.
Humans spend years chasing peace.
Cats wake up with it!
Leota was funny, practical, a little eccentric, and deeply hopeful. The six alley cats knew it.
They also knew she spent far too much time wandering through yesterday and worrying about tomorrow.
Cats don't do that.
Cats don't learn Laundromat Zen.
They arrive already knowing it.
Humans spend years chasing peace.
Cats wake up with it.

Every morning they stretched, yawned, admired the sunshine, and expected breakfast. Every evening they wandered the Big City, returning with another curious treasure—a feather, a button, a marble, a ribbon, a bottle cap, or some other forgotten little thing.

"Look," they seemed to say. "The world is still full of surprises."
They never argued with Leota.

They never told her to get over the past. Instead, they kept bringing her pieces of the present.

Little by little, without realizing it, Leota began looking forward to seeing what the cats would bring home next. And that, the six cats agreed, that the first lesson of Laundromat Zen was learning to widen one's world.

Every morning they watched Leota walk across the street to the Laund-O-Rama.

Every evening they watched her come home again.

Day after day.

Week after week.

Month after month.

The routine suited Leota.

It did not suit the cats.

They had once been alley cats—wanderers, explorers, scavengers, philosophers of rooftops and back fences. They knew every shortcut, every bakery that dropped scraps, every fish market worth visiting, and every warm steam grate in the Big City.

Now they had full stomachs, soft beds, and ears rubbed so often they were in danger of becoming respectable.

The cats were grateful.

But they were also bored.

Leota, they decided, had become stuck.

So they made a plan.

Instead of bringing home feathers and bottle caps, they began bringing home clues.

A bus ticket. Half a road map.

A postcard from a town Leota had never heard of.

A tourist brochure with a waterfall on the front.

A luggage tag.

YES?
CAT
ZEN

A matchbook from a little café two hundred miles
away.
Every day they proudly laid their discoveries at
Leota's feet.
She smiled.
She thanked them.
Then she tucked the curious treasures into a
shoebox and walked across the street to the Laund-
O-Rama.
The cats sighed.
Humans, they agreed, could be wonderfully kind.
But they could also be astonishingly slow learners.

One spring morning, Leota stood in the doorway of
the Laund-O-Rama and looked around.
Everything was just as she had dreamed.
The city had honored her for her work.
People came from miles away to wash their clothes
with Leota's Hopeful Laundry Soap.
The laundromat hummed with laughter, clean
clothes, and the comforting smell of lavender.
Business was thriving.
There was money in the bank.
The cats were well fed.
The customers smiled when she walked through the
door.
By every measure anyone could think of, Leota had
arrived.
She had reached the very top of Laundromat
Mountain.
So why, she wondered, did her feet keep wanting to
walk?

That evening the six cats wandered off on their nightly adventures, disappearing over fences, rooftops, and alley walls as though the whole world belonged to them.
Leota watched until the last tail disappeared into the twilight.
Then she smiled.
The cats had been trying to tell her all along.
They had never stopped wandering.
Perhaps she had never been meant to stop either.
For the first time in years, she thought about her family—not with sadness, not with anger, but with understanding.
They had been nomads in their own way.
Always moving.
Always searching.
She had spent years believing she'd left that part of herself behind.
She hadn't.
She had simply given it a place to rest for a while.
The Laund-O-Rama had healed her.
It had taught her Laundromat Zen.
Now it was teaching her the final lesson.
Sometimes the best thing you can do...
is leave something behind with a light heart before life tells you it's time.
Leota looked at the six cats as they came home beneath the moon.
"I think," she whispered, "it's time we widened our world again."
The cats weren't the least bit surprised.
They'd already packed.

Courage!
Purple Heart
Cat

But first, Leota went home. To the home she left
behind. She took the bus to the outskirts of the city
where her family had lived.
The little shack was gone.
The homemade stove was gone.
The snowball bushes had disappeared.
The clothesline had long since rotted away.
There was only an empty lot full of weeds left.
She asked an old woman sweeping her porch.
"Do you remember the family that lived on that
empty lot?"
The woman thinks.
"Oh...the wanderers?"
"Yes."
"They moved on years ago."
"Do you know where?"
The old woman shakes her head.
"They were never much for staying."
Leota thanked her. The woman turned her back
and went on sweeping.
Leota didn't cry.
She simply stood there a long while.
Then she noticed...
the wild pink rose growing through an nearby old
fence. Just like the rose her sister once handed her.
That's all she needed. Not answers.
Just a blessing from a lost family.
A good memory.
A brave little dandelion.
Sometimes you don't find the people you go looking
for. Sometimes you find the person who went
looking...

Leota returned home and bought the Laund-O-Rama
from the son of the very man who had first hired her
years before.
For the first time in her life, the little laundromat
belonged to her.
Then she hired Mr. Hays as caretaker.
Mr. Hays had always been the maintenance man.
Quiet. Widowed. Dependable. He could repair
anything from a broken dryer to a squeaky door. He
never hurried. His shoes were always polished, and
he believed every washing machine had a
personality.
"A washing machine is like people," he said. "Usually
tells you what's wrong before it breaks."
Leota thought that sounded true of hearts, too.
One rainy afternoon, while customers sat watching
the dryers turn and turn, Leota sighed.
"Waiting is the hardest part of laundry."
Mr. Hays smiled.
"So don't wait."
"What do people do instead?"
"They dance."
Leota laughed.
"You tango?"
"I used to."
The very next week, a little hand-painted sign
appeared beside the change machine.
**FREE TANGO LESSSONS DURING THE WASH
CYCLE**
Beginners Welcome
At first, everyone laughed.

WHO,
CAT ZEN
ME?
WHO,

Then one brave grandmother stood up.
A retired truck driver joined her.
A little girl copied their footsteps.
Soon husbands were dancing with wives, neighbors
with neighbors, strangers with strangers. Children
twirled between laundry baskets while the dryers
hummed and the washers swished.
The six alley cats watched the whole affair with
considerable skepticism.
They agreed that humans had entirely too many feet.
Still...
The Laund-O-Rama became known as the happiest
laundromat in the Big City.
People came to wash their clothes.
Leota smiled every time she heard laughter rising
above the hum of the machines.
And soon, every Wednesday evening, after the last
load was done, Mr. Hays cleared the folding tables.
Someone brought cookies.
Someone made coffee.
They danced.
Later, since Leota studied the cello...
The dryers thump.
The washers swish.
Mr. Hays taps a wrench.
Someone plays harmonica.
The laundromat becomes an accidental orchestra.
People come because they know someone will listen.
They want to be happy.
Mr. Hays fixes machines.
Leota fixes discouraged hearts.

The cats supervise.
No one advertised it.
It simply became known.
Leota insisted the six cats join the party. The cats
hated tango.
Every time people started dancing, six cats scattered
in six directions.
One leaps into an empty dryer.
One sits on top of the change machine looking
horrified.
One bats at a shoelace.
One refuses to participate because, in the cat's
opinion,
**"Cats perfected graceful movement centuries ago.
Humans are merely trying to catch up."**
The rest hide under tables.

The End

9 798987 202715